MW00901205

For Noah & Jonah

Bear and Panda Have a Picnic!
written and illustrated by Mari Santiago

Bear and Panda Have a Picnic!

One day, Bear spotted a creature he had never seen before. She had white fur with black ears, arms, legs, and eye patches.

"What kind of bear are you?" asked Bear.

"I'm a panda, silly!" Panda replied. "Would you like to share my peanut butter toast?"

"That's my favorite food!" said Bear.
He gobbled it up in three bites.

After talking awhile, they realized that they weren't so different after all.

They were both bear-shaped, even though they were different colors.

They both liked to watch scary movies.
Sometimes they were **too** scary for Panda.

They both liked catching snowflakes in jars...

...and they both liked card games, even though Panda frowned when Bear won.

They both dreamt of far-away adventures...

...and they both believed in dandelion wishes.

Bear yawned as the sun set beneath the hills.

"It's about time for a snooze!" he said.
"Let's have a picnic again tomorrow!"

As soon as Bear arrived home, the phone rang.

"Brrr! It's much colder here than where I'm from," said a chilly Panda voice.

"Don't worry!" said Bear.
"I can make the cold disappear!"

And he did.

the end

six

four

eight

Made in the USA
Middletown, DE
26 January 2021